FREEWAY

Thoughts Reflections and Observation- Finding
room Enough to Evaluate who You Are

PEDRO TWEED

Printed in the United States of America.

Library of Congress Control Number: 2007900554

ISBN	Paperback	978-1-68536-410-6
	eBook	978-1-68536-411-3

Westwood Books Publishing LLC
Atlanta Financial Center
3343 Peachtree Rd NE Ste 145-725
Atlanta, GA 30326

www.westwoodbookspublishing.com

CONTENTS

To all my gymnasts, former and new,
this book was inspired by all of you. I love you.

ACKNOWLEDGEMENTS

This book is dedicated to so many people that if I mention them all, it will be another book by itself. So if you don't see your name in here, please understand that I still thought of you.

First to my mother, Cleopatra
Thanks for raising me the way you did and instilling in me the strong values that made me who I am today. I love you.

To My wife, Crystal Tweed.
Thanks for being the most supportive wife in the world.

To my brother Luis, a.k.a. Northstar
I'm so proud of you and your music; you are going to change the world.

To my daughters
Amanda Tweed
Since the moment you were born, you continue to bring me joy. Thank you for pushing me to get the book out. I will always love you.

Devin Hayes-Tweed
Don't ever forget you were chosen with love.

And Lindsay, Stephanie, Katrina
I only been your father for a short time but
I will love you for a long time

To my friends
Dr. Rosa, The Novogrodsky, Caroline, Luis, Brian, Steve, Angelo,
Joe, Andy, Woldek, Sisco, Ben, Rob, Mike V. George, Arlen,
Nancy, Lisa, Margaret, Ellen, Crystal, The Garns, Perry, Denise,
The Conatys, The Brasingtons, Jasmin, Pat, Conor, and Eliot.
Thank you for believing in me.

FREEWAY

A Metaphor for Life

I'm going to assume that if you are going on the freeway, you already have a vehicle. Hopefully, when you go on the freeway, you already have a destination. If you have never been where you're going, then make sure you get directions. When you go on the freeway, you see many entrances and exits; but it is up to you to decide which one will be more beneficial for you to take in order to reach your destination. There are signs on the freeway; these signs provide us with information to help us reach our destination easier. There are two types of signs: external and internal.

External signs are the ones that tell us where we are right now or how far we are from our destination.

Internal signs are the ones that tell us what's going on inside. For example, the gauge in our cars that lets us know how much fuel we have or the oil indicator that warns us if we are out of oil.

Success in life is pretty much like going on the freeway. (In fact, some people say that life is a trip.) First, the vehicle is you. Then we set a destination, which is any task, goal, or skill that you wish to achieve. Whatever it is, that is your destination. Once you've decided on the destination, you get directions; and by that I mean instruction, advice, or information from someone that has done or is currently doing or teaching the career, goal, or skill you wish to achieve.

When you get going on your task, there will be signs, but be careful because signs often come disguised as coincidences. For example, you decided that you want to become a schoolteacher; and you keep meeting schoolteachers. Okay, so maybe that's not a good example because if you want to become a schoolteacher, you have to go to school; and the school is full of teachers. You may have heard the saying "When the student is ready, the teacher will appear." But what I really want you to be ready for is the ability to recognize these signs when they appear. Just like the signs on the freeway, they are not to be ignored because the way you follow the signs is going to determine whether you are going to succeed or not.

Keep in mind that signs are not always the bearers of good news. But don't worry because no matter what the sign says, you have the power to change it. As I stated earlier, there are two types of signs: external and internal.

In life, external signs are the ones that come from outside of us, like other people, books, television, etc. Sometimes these signs direct us to the right path but sometimes they don't.

Internal signs are very important because they are the ones that provide us with the fuel necessary to reach our goals. This fuel comes in the form of our internal conversations and desires. In other words, our thoughts; and just like the signs in our car, these are the signs that tell us if we have enough fuel to reach our destination. The way we think determines if our tank will be full or empty. Negative thinking empties the tank, while positive thinking fills the tank. Strong desire is high-grade fuel.

Sometimes in our travels, we may miss our signs and our exits. But that's okay. Because as long as we are driving, we have the option of taking the next exit, turn back, and get back on track.

SIMPLE ANSWER, SIMPLE QUESTION

Often we ask ourselves why,
But the answer is always because.
But if we accept everything as it is,
There will be no question of why.
And because there is no question of why
There is no answer, just because.

It is what it is just because it is.
To wonder why the sky is blue is indeed
A waste of time and appreciation of its beauty.
I'd rather enjoy the beautiful sky by looking at it.
The enjoyment of life is in the participation of life,
Not in wondering how life works.
The *how* is something that we will learn through the experience
of living it.
I'd rather learn how to press play on the disk player and enjoy the
music
Than to wonder how the light inside makes it play.
After all, the enjoyment is in listening.

TEACHER TO STUDENT

Don't rush; I will guide you through a dark tunnel, which I have already traveled. But when we get halfway and you see the light at the other end, do not assume that you could now make it on your own. Because I alone know where the rest of the lumps, bumps, and holes are since I've traveled that dark tunnel many times before.

Don't rush, because anything that is great and worthwhile appreciates in time.

Don't give up; in order to give, you must first have. You can't give something that you don't have, so you have to get it first before you give it up.

YIN AND YANG

For everything that is first, there is a last.
For everything that is backward, there is a forward.
For every large quantity, there is a small opportunity.
For everything that is evolving there is revolving.
For every right question, there is a wrong answer.
For every wrong question, there is a right answer.
A complete day has light and darkness
A complete circle has a forward and a backward.
Harmony has a low and a high.
There is no complete circle without going back to its origin.

In the principles of yin and yang, it is believed that the law of nature is two complete opposites working together to achieve balance. One of the examples I like to give my students so they understand better is that of riding a bike. In order to complete the task, you have to press and release. The thing about riding a bike is that you must be in balance. Just the same, in order to enjoy your ride in life longer, you must be in motion. It doesn't work if you just sit there. Another thing about yin and yang is that it suggests that bad and good could not exist without each other. This is good news because when you think that everything is going bad for you, you can look for the good.

PEOPLE ACCORDING TO THE ELEMENTS

Fire
These are people that are selfish and do not care about anyone but themselves. They usually think that they have the answer to everything. When they're around, they usually make people feel very uncomfortable or hot under the collar if you will.

Wood
These are people that have very low self-esteem and are sometimes hollow inside. They are mainly led by other elements. In other words, they are mainly followers.

Water
These people are used by everyone and then pushed aside but are always kept at arm's length just in case.

Wind
These are people that are nosey and are always there; gossip makes them stronger. They like to stir up things and, push aside anyone that gets in their way.

Earth
These are people that are stepped on, but these are also people that hold people up.

When I first wrote this, I was only sixteen; and back then, I had no knowledge of Chinese medicine. This is in no way related. These are just thoughts.

DIRECTION

In one of my less busier weekends, I was in two different competitions at two different locations. One of them was at Chappaqua, New York and the other one was at Long Island the next day.

I needed to save as much time as possible because the next day competition would start very early in the morning. So I went to one of the coaches from Long Island and asked him if he could tell me the quickest way to get to Long Island from Chappaqua. He replied, "Dude, you came to the right place because I have the best direction in the world."

He sounded very enthusiastic and very confident with what he was saying. So I got excited because if there was anything I wanted that day, it was the best direction in the world. He proceeded to tell me the absolute and fastest way he thought I can get to Long Island from Chappaqua; but while he was telling me this, there was another coach that was also from Long Island standing next to us who overheard what he was saying and totally disagreed. He said, "Dude, why are you sending him the long way?"

"That's not the long way, Coach," the first coach answered back.

This started a debate that lasted for about half an hour, as what I've heard the next day from one of the coaches standing nearby who witnesses the whole thing. You see, they became so enraged in proving to each other that their particular direction was the best one that they did not notice that I left and asked someone else.

The moral of the story is that the directions you choose should be the one that you truly believe is the best for you, no matter what road someone else takes for himself or herself. You must be passionate about your chosen direction in life.

Although the two coaches had different directions, they both believed that their way was the easiest. All I'm saying is that when you have direction, your travels in life are easier, but that does not mean that you won't get lost once in a while. As a matter of fact, you will; but if you have direction, you'll get back on track.

The thing to remember is that he who has no direction is not going anywhere.

VALUE

I've always wondered who gave a piece of rock their value and why is one rock more valuable than another. Who decided that?

To me, no explanation will suffice. You just don't know how many times I've heard people ask when looking at a ring, "Is that real? It looks real."

You see, what I don't understand is if you can't tell that it is real with the naked eye, then why buy a "real" expensive one in the first place. No one can tell unless they put it under a microscope; and let me tell you, there are not too many people walking around with one. What is even more ridiculous is getting jewels to put on a safe and never use them. I think that we have it backward and we are placing value on the wrong things.

It seems like the value we put on things keeps going up while the value we put on people keeps going down. Some of the biggest TV shows of the past few years have been the ones that put people down, in other words, devalued them. Some people justify this rudeness by telling us that they are just saying what we are all thinking inside but don't have the guts to say. Well, I have the guts to say this: if everyone is thinking this way, check please. I want to get off.

Entertainment is heading on a downward spiral where people are becoming famous for being rude. Remember when Regis had the game show *Who Wants To Be a Millionaire?* At that time, it was the top-rated show on television. The show was egged out by another game show called *The weakest link*. The interesting thing about this was that the show's success was largely because the host was good at insulting the contestants.

My question is when will it stop? How far do we have to go before someone really loses their mind? Okay, am I being too harsh? After all, we are accepting this behavior in the name of fun. So I have to ask, what is it about us that we are willing to accept other people's misery as a form of entertainment?

My theory is that we don't even value ourselves. We think of ourselves as less than others, and some people that market this stuff know it. Some don't even try to hide it. If you go to a bookstore, you'll see books on the shelves with covers saying "for Dummies or Idiots." We go and buy them as of to admit, "Yes, I'm a dummy. I need that book."

The problem is that when we don't value ourselves, we don't value other people, and we begin to accept irresponsibility in the name of fun, and we become more and more desensitized, and we go further and further without realizing that someone is getting hurt, and the worst thing is that we are passing this on to the ones we should value the most: our children.

SMOKING

If you looked at a $60,000 car, the body looks in perfect condition. But then the car drove away, and you saw a lot of smoke coming out of it. You would you think that there's something wrong with that car.

If you passed by a house and you saw a lot of smoke coming out of it, you would think that there's something wrong.

If you were cooking and you saw a lot of smoke coming out of the oven, you would think that there's something wrong.

That's why when I see smoke coming out of people, I always wonder, what's wrong?

JUDGMENT DAY

It was a hot summer day, and I was not feeling too well. My gymnasts, my coaches, and I went to the lake for the rest of the day. We thought it would be a good idea if we went and cooled off.

When we arrived there, I began to notice something. The kids and the coaches were whispering things between them without including me. I became a little paranoid because they kept looking at me while they were whispering. So I knew that they were talking about me. I started to get more and more angry, especially because one of the coaches and I were dating, and she was keeping me out of it, and she looked as if she was the main culprit.

I decided go to her and confront her. I was going to ask her, "How dare you go and whisper things about me! What is wrong with you? Can't you see I'm looking right at you? I can tell that you are talking about me. It is so obvious."

As I started moving toward them, they went into a huddle as if they were not going to let me in. This further infuriated me. When I got closer, they opened up and sang "Happy Birthday" to me.

After that incident, I wondered how many times in the past I may have had passed judgment on people and assumed that they were thinking something about me and I was totally wrong.

Once I was sitting at dinner, and a beautiful girl was looking at me. She was smiling and giggling. She even leaned over to her friend and told her about me; this I knew because she pointed right at me when she talked to her. There was no doubt that this girl thought I was hot. What more could I ask for? I decided to make my move and go talk to her. I did not want to blow this. But how could I? She already made all the signs. All I had to do was seal the deal, so I said to her, "I noticed that you were looking at me and smiling."

She said, "Yes, you have snot on your nose."

What I learned from both of these situations is that we should never pass judgment on people just based on their behavior. In both of these stories, I was dead wrong. But it was the way I was thinking or what I wanted to believe that made the difference, not what was actually going on.

What if on the first story I decided to believe that what they were whispering about me were good things? What if on the second story I chose to believe that the reason they were looking at me was a bad thing? I would have been right on both occasions, but it would not have been any more satisfying than when I was wrong both times. The idea is to expect the best every time, regardless of the situation. Think of every situation as a favorable one for you.

SUCCESS

Success can be summed up in two words: practice and intent. If we couple these two words together, success is sure to come. If we separate them, success may or may not come; and if it does, it will come slowly.

You could have all the intention in the world to reach success; but without practice, it is just a dream. Wake up.

You could show up to practice everyday; but if you practice without the intention to get better, it will be just like walking on a treadmill—your feet are moving, but you are not going anywhere. Don't get me wrong. There are benefits in walking on the treadmill. But if your intention is to move forward, you are wasting your time.

Earlier I said that if we couple these two words together, you are sure to reach success. This is what I meant by that:

Make your intent to practice success, and practice with the intent to succeed.

Intent + Practice = Success

Practice with the intent to improve every time.

15

BALANCE

True balance is the ability to remain steady in an unsteady situation.

Standing on two feet is easy; but if I ask you to stand on one leg without moving, that will be a little more challenging. What if I ask you to stand on one leg on a pole and you remain steady without moving? Then everyone will agree that you have great balance. What if someone started to shake that pole and you still remain steady? Then everyone will marvel at your balance.

You see, balance is not only when things are going good and things are easy—that is, standing on two feet. Balance is when things are not easy and are not going well and you find the ability to remain unchanged, unmoved, and steady.

Real balance is when you have an overflow of the good and you learn to use it to correct some of the bad. It is also the ability to find the good when bad things are happening.

Simply said, balance is trying to make things even when they are uneven. It is taking away when there's too much and adding more when there's too little.

To exemplify it best, take a look at the scale of justice. In order to get it to balance, you must either add or take away.

The one thing that offsets balance are people that are extremists. I believe that any two opposites taken to an extreme will automatically arrive at the same conclusion. For example, if you go to a mall and you see a group of guys standing, looking at female. If an extremely beautiful girl passes by them, you may hear something like this:

"Wow! Did you see that?"; and if an extremely unattractive girl passes by, you'll hear the same thing: "Wow! Did you see that?"

Another example I like to use is that of the rain and the sun—two complete opposites. But you could protect yourself from both with the same thing: an umbrella. Furthermore, if you see a person who is extremely good and he goes around kissing everyone he sees, you may assume that he is crazy. If you see someone who's extremely bad and he goes around hitting everyone he sees, you will arrive at the same conclusion.

And so are extremists that cause disharmony and are willing to kill others that don't believe in their cause.

DESTINATION

Is where you are right now your destination, or was it your destiny?

Some people like to say that life is a journey, not a destination. I like to think that life is a whole bunch of mini-destinations. I think that people who think of life as just a journey are in for quite a long trip. I don't know about you, but I always get nervous when someone is taking a journey with me and don't know where they're going.

My limited understanding of this is that our destination is our own choosing, and destiny is chosen by a power greater than us. I like to believe that we have much better control over something that we chose. So I choose destination.

The problem with destiny is that it is often set too far in the future or is discovered too late. In movies like *Stars Wars*, you may hear Yoda say things like "It is your destiny, Young Luke." Or you may hear someone say to you "It was your destiny" after you've achieved something.

The thing with destination is that it is more immediate and it could be handled by you. You don't need a guru or a psychic to tell you where you are going; all you really need is a goal and a map.

Setting a destination is simple. All you have to do is make a decision, a decision to change where you are right now to where you want to go. I'm hoping and believing that since you do choose your destination, you are choosing a better place than where you are now.

Whether your destination is to be a better coach, a better parent, a better teacher, or make more money, it doesn't matter what it is as long as you get to choose what you want to make better.

If you want to know the truth, embark on a destination, and you'll arrive at your destiny.

FEELINGS AND EMOTIONS

Feelings and emotions are the steering wheels to our destiny. The better we handle them, the easier the trip. However, keep in mind that a steering wheel has no intelligence of its own, just like our emotions; and since it has no intelligence, the steering wheel has to be directed by us. Just like our emotions, steering wheels have no real power by themselves, and neither do our emotions. Since they have no power of their own, emotions are only as real as we allow them to be. The problem is that they present themselves as real, and we respond to them as if they are real. We harbor our emotion in our mind, and our mind does not know how to differentiate between what's real and what's not. For example, if you went to see a scary movie, your body and your emotions will respond as if it is real; but we both know that it is not real. The trick is to recognize the emotions and expose them for the impostors that they are. Unfortunately, what often happens is that we get caught up in believing our emotions, and we let our emotions overrule our intelligence. When that happens, we do and say irrational things. Think about it. How many times have you said something you regretted based on the way you were feeling at that moment? I dare say that most of the mistakes we make are made on an emotional level, not on a rational and intelligent level.

Remember I said handle your emotions; I did not say hold on to them. One of the biggest mistakes we make is that we hold on to an emotion for too long. A friend of mine was holding on to the same emotion for over four years, and I kept saying to him, "You have to let go." Because what I saw was that the longer he held on to that emotion, the more pain it caused him. What he did not understand is that the bigger the curveball life throws at you on the road to your destiny, the more you have to let go of the steering wheel in order to make the new adjustment.

We get into problems when we let our emotions go unchecked and we let them escalate to the point where we crash; and after that, it is too late.

Handling the steering wheel is not easy, especially when there is traffic—in other words, a lot of thoughts. But what makes it even more complicated is a thing that I like to call *taking off your coat*.

This is when you get in your car and start driving, and then you feel uncomfortable. In order to be comfortable, you start to take off your coat but continue driving; and you let the person on the passenger seat take over the wheel (emotions).

The thing is that if you hand over the control (your emotion) to someone else, then you can't hold him or her responsible for what they do with it. The best part about this metaphor is that in real life, after we take off our jackets, we usually take the control back.

All I'm trying to say is that in life, there are going to be times when you are on your way and other people are going to cut you off. Some are going to flip you the bird; some are going to curse you out. Ultimately, the only thing that matters is not what happens outside of you but how you handle the steering wheel that's inside.

OUTSTANDING

When I went to the community college here in my town, I took one of the hardest classes. I knew it was hard because every student at the college said so and I believed them. They (the students) said that only 10 % of the class passed, and I should not even bother taking it. After hearing this, I became a little concerned, and I went to get advice from two of my favorite teachers at the school, Mr. and Mrs. Grace. I told them what I've heard about the class I wanted to take, and Mrs. Grace simply replied, "Well, I guess you are going to have to be in that 10 %, aren't you?"

After the semester was over, I could not hold back my joy. I went looking for Mr. Grace to tell him the news.

"Mr. Grace, I'm in the top 5 %of the class," I said.

He looked at me; and as he shook my hand, he said, "Outstanding, young man."

Outstanding. That word made me so happy that I began to use it anytime I had a chance. It became part of my everyday vocabulary. I became obsessed with finding people that did something outstanding just so I could use the word. I used it at work with my gymnastic students every time they did something good or got a new skill.

Years later, I was watching a television show. You know, one of those magazine shows where they were showing a research done with teens. What they did was put seven teens in one room, and six of them were told to give the wrong answers to a series of simple questions. The one being tested, not knowing that the others were planted, will continuously give the wrong answers even though he knew the right answers just to go along with the rest. "OUTSTANDING," I said to myself. What this young man didn't know is that outstanding people become outstanding because they stand out from the rest. Unfortunately, the teens today are exactly that way. They feel that they have to conform to the status quo; and they have to act, dress, and be like everyone else. Look, I'm not saying that you can't dress like everyone else. I dressed like everyone else when I went to school; I had to wear a uniform. Otherwise, the nun will be very upset. My point is that in order to be outstanding, it is the right performance that counts. The Yankees all wear the same uniform; but when they play, we look at the performance of the players, good or bad. But I guarantee you one thing: no one is trying to strike out because the person before just did.

Being outstanding is the ability to choose the right performance even though the group is going a different way. Don't get confused; I'm not saying that in order to be outstanding you have to do something different than the rest of the pack. In fact, there are situations in life, sports or whatever, where you have to do exactly what the others are doing. But in order to be outstanding, you have to have the right performance. For example, a race car driver has to go on the same path as everyone else, but it is the performance he gives that makes him stand out from the rest. OUTSTANDING.

I REST MY CASE

I flew
Because I cut all the negativity from my
mind that was weighting me down.

I ran
Because I was free from those thoughts that were holding me back.

I cried
Because I woke up to reality and realized that the world was cruel.

I loved
Because I believed that was the only way to change it.

I labored
Because I believed that this may be true.

But I rest
On the laurels that God is in charge.

I WANT YOU; I REALLY, REALLY WANT YOU

A friend of mine was having trouble with his girlfriend; he felt that she just wasn't as attentive as she used to be. He recalled that she used to tell him "I love you" all the time, and the one thing that he really missed was that she used to say "I want you" all the time.

I told him not to feel bad or take it personally because all relationships start out that way, and then after a while, we take each other for granted, and we don't say those nice things as often as we used to.

Not convinced, he looked at me and said, "But I loved it when she said 'I want you,' and she does not say it anymore."

Well, my friends, I'm here to tell you that that's not true. She was telling him. He just wasn't noticing.

So I took the liberty of making a list to show him how many times she said "I want you":

I want you to take out the garbage.
I want you to take me out to dinner.
I want you to buy me a car.
I want you to buy me a house.
I want you to take me on vacation.
I want you to take me shopping.
And I want you to believe that I don't want you for you money.

HAVING AN AFFAIR

I was telling a friend of mine about something I was planning to do for my girlfriend—a big surprise for her birthday. After I finished telling her what I was planning, she said to me, "Wow! That's quite an affair. She is a lucky lady."

But with my limited understanding of the English language back then, I really didn't understand fully what that word meant. But judging from her reaction, I imagined that what it meant was that if it was big, took a lot of planning, and you wanted everyone to know, that's an affair.

I quickly came home and couldn't wait to call my girlfriend and tell her the great news and to impress her with the use of my newly found English phrase, so I proudly said, "Honey, I'm having an affair!"

You know, as a speaker, I will stop right here for a moment and let you conjure all kinds of images in your head as to what happened next. But as a writer, I have to fill the rest of the page, so here we go.

As you may have imagined, things didn't go quite as I expected. There was a long silence on the other end of the line, which was finally broken by this question: "HOW CAN YOU DO THAT TO ME?"

I was in shock. I couldn't understand why she sounded so angry like I did something wrong; after all, I thought I was doing a good thing. So I said to her, "Honey, I'm doing it for you."

"For me," she said. "Whatever gave you that idea?"

"The girl that taught me these words told me that this was one of the nicest things I could do for you."

How am I supposed to know that these three little words that are exactly the same have completely opposite meanings?

The thing is that although they have different meanings, they do have a similarity beyond the spelling—they both start out in secrecy and they both take planning. But the major difference of course is that one brings about shame while the other one brings happiness.

The key is that if the affair you are having is not one that you can proudly shout out from the top of your lungs to the world, then it is not worth having.

I SEE YOU

I see you when you say hello and wave your pride on your face.

You think I don't; but don't worry, I see you.

When you put your fist up and show your solidarity with your brothers.

You think I don't; but don't worry, I see you.

When you give and take to your brothers, but you don't want anyone to know but them.

Don't worry, I see you.

When you show up to community meetings to show your support for your people.

Don't worry, I see you.

You see, you fool most people, and most people don't see who you really are.

But don't worry, I see you.

How could you

Put your fist up and say you love your race, when you are responsible for destroying your race?

How could you

Believe that you are helping your race when you can't even be proud of yourself?

You don't have to hide what you do if you are proud of it.

And don't worry, I know that when you give and take to your brothers,

You give them drugs and you take their money.

But it's more than that; you are also taking their minds and destroying your race. You see, you think I don't; but I see you.

THE PERFECT MAN

The perfect man of today has to be like Superman: able to pay all things with a single check, able to travel anywhere their mate desires at the speed of light, able to take sharp comments without getting hurt, and able to show sensitivity without appearing wimpy. He is also able to have a job, but not one that makes you spend too much time away from the family. He is able to cook, do the dishes, and take out the garbage.

The chief complaint of a woman today is that housework is tough and that men don't help around the house. Another one is that the man doesn't spend enough time at home. My question for the modern (I don't cook or clean) woman is that if a man is doing all that, then what is left for you to do? Don't answer that. I know: go shopping.

The problem is that today many young ladies engage into relationships with that unrealistic expectation, making it very difficult for any hardworking young man who loves them but doesn't make a six-figure income to fulfill these expectations. At the same time, a man who's working hard on the financial end has been saying that he does not have enough time to spend at home because he is too busy working.

What these young ladies don't understand is that no human can live up to that ideal. Even God Almighty rested on the seventh day. Jesus died on the cross, and kryptonite will kill Superman.

THE TRUTH

"The truth hurts," people say proudly, but the reality is that it shouldn't. Oh, it may cause some bumps and bruises initially; but when you get to the understanding of the real meaning of the truth, it does not hurt. In fact, it is liberating. After all, the other side of the coin in this cliché is "The truth will set you free."

Usually when you hear people that are caught up using this term, they use it in an accusatory way. They usually say things like this, "The truth hurts, doesn't it?" As if the revelation they just made about you is something you did not know. What these idiots don't realize is that the realization they just made is their perception of what they believe you are, not who you really are.

The only way that it could hurt is if you begin to agree with them. You may ask yourself, "What if the things they are saying are true?" Then it should be liberating, not hurtful. If it is something that you don't like about yourself, be grateful that you are not fooling anyone and take the appropriate measures to change that undesirable behavior. However, if their truth is not your truth and you know that they are just doing it to be hurtful, then you must take the appropriate measures and reevaluate your relationship with those individuals.

Unfortunately, what we do is give too much time and energy to people who tell lies about us. We become hurt and obsessed and allow them to occupy too much space in our heads. We do that by questioning and second-guessing ourselves, asking things like "How could they say that about me? Are they right about me?" I've been guilty of this many times, instead of realizing that the fact that I found

29

out who these people really are is actually beneficial to me. Because now I know that I definitely don't want those types of people around me. Besides, don't worry because the truth will always surface to the top.

This is the way I illustrated it to my martial arts students.

If you and I went to the lake and saw the reflection of the moon on the water, and just as we started to admire the true beauty of nature someone passes by and starts to throw pebbles on the lake, without a doubt, that will distort the true reflection of the moon on the lake, and we will not be able to see a clear reflection of the moon. But eventually, the person will get tired of throwing pebbles, and the water will settle, and we will once again see the true reflection of the moon. But even that does not matter because if you look up, you'll realize that the real moon has remained undisturbed.

Just like that, when people are throwing pebbles at you (telling lies and half-truths), put your head up, and you will see that the real you will remain undisturbed.

PEOPLE DON'T SUCCEED

People don't succeed because . . .

Instead of searching for answers, they search for excuses.

People don't succeed because . . .

Instead of taking full responsibility for their actions, they delegate blame.

People don't succeed because . . .

Instead of spending time searching for what's right, they spend it defending what's wrong.

LOYALTY

True loyalty is when what you say behind me and what you say in front of me are exactly the same.

The only difference between the words "loyalty" and "royalty" is the exchange of the letter *L* for the letter *R*. The *L* would stand for "liars" and "losers" and the *R* for "respect" and "reverence."

I say this because people that are disloyal usually lie, and that makes them losers, and I believe that when you are loyal to someone, you should treat him or her with the same respect that you will treat royalty.

We all know that there's a set of ethics and rules that we have to follow when we meet royalty; but there should be another set of ethics on how to be loyal to our friends, wives, girlfriends, boyfriends, teachers, coaches, and anyone who at one time or another helped enrich our lives but somehow our egos got in the way and we forgot.

What is interesting to me is that some people are willing to bow and curtsy for someone they just met and never touched in their lives but are not willing to show the same respect for someone that has. I've learned through experience that after a period of time together, people begin to take each other for granted. This to me is sad because like everything else, the value of a person should increase with time. Some people are so focused on the new that they forget the old may have the same or sometimes more value. But what we need to do is be like an artist who is creating a masterpiece. He works very close to it; and every once in a while, he has to take a step back in order to really see what he is doing. We need to do the same: take a step back and take a really good look so we could learn to appreciate better what we already have.

Yes, it is true. People that are disloyal may have the ability to lie right to your face. But remember this, the ones they lie to the most are themselves.

QUESTIONS AND ANSWERS

Q. What makes you better?
A. My search for quality.

Q. What makes you good?
A. My discovery of what is bad.

Q. What makes you sane?
A. My search for love.

Q. What makes you insane?
A. When I find it.

HOW TO TELL IF YOUR FIANCÉE NO LONGER CARES

If blood is dripping from your face and she's more concerned about the blood on the floor than she is about what happened to your face.

There's a good chance she may no longer care about you.

If you get sick and your fiancée buys vitamin C for somebody else and nothing for you.

There's a good chance she may no longer care about you.

If she believes that going out to bars with other guys is more important than saving a relationship with you.

There's a good chance she may no longer care about you.

If you go to a restaurant and she believes that flirting with the waiter in front of you is okay and it should not bother you.

There's a good chance she may no longer care about you.

If you marked yes to any or all of these statements, there's a good chance you are not getting married.

SPEED

The first thing that a state trooper says to you when he pulls you over is, "Do you know how fast you were going?"

I always think to myself, "Why is he asking me that question? He is the one with the radar." The obvious answer will probably be "a little too fast." That will be my guess. But for some reason, sarcasm never works too well with cops. So I kept my thoughts to myself, but while I was there in my head, I thought that his question made no sense because he already knew the answer. But beyond that, I kept thinking about how people have a huge fascination with speed. They are always concerned with measuring how fast we could do things as if nothing else matters.

They want faster cars, faster computers, fast food, and fast women. We are now living in a microwave mentality world, a world that is more concerned with speed than they are about practicality. People don't realize that the important thing is not how fast we do things but having the right timing and accuracy.

Throwing a fastball at 110 miles per hour doesn't mean a thing if it doesn't cross home plate. Arriving on time is more important than arriving half an hour early but unprepared.

Besides, what's all the hoopla? Speed is relative anyway. It depends on who, how, where, or when.

Remember, back in the days (as the kids today will say), we used to stand in front of a conventional oven, and it was just fine. Then the invention of the microwave came along, and we thought that it was fast, and then after a while, we stood in front of it, asking it to hurry up. And how many times have you seen someone speeding and pass you by while you were driving, and then later on, you see them on the side of the road stopped by a state trooper?

You see, my friend, trying to do things faster than they should be done is not always a good thing. Quite often, it could lead to sloppy work, and it could also be dangerous. Remember that in life we have three stages: we are born, we live, and we die. What is your hurry? Take your time and enjoy the ride. And for those men who still don't agree with me, just go and ask any woman, and they will tell you that two minutes is just too fast.

BAD BOYS

They say that when a young woman looks for love, she looks for someone just like her dad. So you could imagine my surprise when I asked my daughter, who I think is a sensible and intelligent young lady, what kind of men she liked. She said, "I like bad boys."

I was shocked because I am the furthest thing from being a bad boy. I kept asking myself, "Why would a smart young lady say something like that?" Then I realized that she was not alone in this sentiment. Most young ladies today are attracted to bad boys. But I didn't really care about that; what I really wanted to find out is why.

One of the things I found is that most young ladies think that they could fix them. Now it does not start out that way, but that is how it ends up. How many times have you heard a young woman complaining about her man and how horrible she is being treated? Then when you ask her why she puts up with that garbage, the common answer is "Because inside, he is really a nice person; and in his own way, I think he really loves me."

The thing is that we only do that with people; we never go to an electronic store and say, "I want a bad television." We never go to a car dealership and say, "Give me the worst car you can find; and don't worry, I can fix it."

Now when my daughter told me she liked bad boys, she was very young; and today, she doesn't even remember saying it. As a matter of fact, she thinks that that was a stupid comment for someone to say, and I'm happy for that, but there are still a lot of ladies, young and old alike, who believe that being with a bad boy is a good idea. This is my advice for all the young ladies on how to pick the right guy:

When you pick a guy, it should be like buying a used car.

First, it must be reliable.

Second, it must work.

Third, the inside must be better than or just as good as the outside.

Fourth, have a mechanic that you trust look at it to make sure it doesn't need fixing.

Fifth, make sure it could go for a long ride.

Sixth, make sure that the title is free and clear and it doesn't belong to someone else.

Look, if you are reading this, I don't know who you are and I don't know your sense of humor. So I don't know if you're reading this with a sense of humor like I meant it, but I'm only half joking because I am serious about this. If you choose a car that does not work, then you are also choosing not to go too far.

Bad boys, bad boys, what are you gonna do when the wrath of a caring father comes down on you?

INTELLIGENCE VERSUS IGNORANCE

In a fictitious world, if intelligence and ignorance have a fight, who will win? I posed that question to many people, and without hesitation, they said intelligence will win. Then I told them that ignorance won, and then they asked me why. I told them because intelligence uses logic and ignorance uses belief; but remember that I said that this is a fictitious world because in the real world, intelligence won't argue with ignorance. Or at least, that's what I want to believe.

But the reality is that sometimes intelligence does engage in an argument with ignorance; and the reason is that no matter how much intelligence does not want to engage in one, it is overruled by an emotion called frustration.

Here is how the bout went round by round.

Round one:

Intelligence comes out full of confidence, prepared, and armed with facts and data. Ignorance stood there rooted on his beliefs. Intelligence threw a right full of photos and evidence; Ignorance ducked, came up, and hit him with a left full of "You must have changed that on Photo Shop!" This stunned Intelligence, sending him to the ground in frustration and conceding the fight.

Have you ever had an argument like that? Where no matter what you say or how much proof you have, people just won't accept it because they confused their ignorance with intelligence?

When I started writing, one of the first things I put down on paper was "If God gave me the power to change one thing in life, what will I change?" My answer was "I will give everyone special eyes so they can see people in the color of their liking." Then I thought that's good but not good enough because there will still be social prejudice. So I changed my mind and wrote intelligence because I believed that if you have intelligence, you have no prejudice, but I was wrong.

I met people that are considered intelligent and have issues with prejudice. You see, prejudice has nothing to do with logic or intelligence; it has to do with emotion. So what we have to do is move beyond the basic level of intelligence to super intelligence.

Super intelligence is when we no longer allow emotions to be the dominant ruler in our mind. It is when we learn to recognize and expose stupidity before we engage in an argument. we educate people by the way we live our lives and showing what works not by telling them but by the example we set.

> Do not shine the light too bright on ignorance because you
> will blind them.
>
> —Pedro

DEPEND ON IT

I was talking to a friend of mine who recently sold her business, citing that there's no dependable help. Another friend told me that his business was suffering because he could not depend on his help. The problem is that this is just not limited to my friends. We all have been afflicted at one time or another by disappointments because we depended on someone, and they let us down. But, let me tell you, it is not only who to depend on but also to depend on what.

How many times have you heard someone say, "I have to get a dependable car"? I was one of those people. One of my favorite songs is the old Doobie Brothers song "Depending on You"; and oddly enough, another one of my other favorite songs is by Santana, "No One to Depend On." The funny thing about these two songs is that although they are complete opposites, this is exactly how it happens in real life.

When you first meet people or hire them, you give them the benefit of the doubt and you depend on them, and then later on, when they disappoint you, you get frustrated, and you begin to say things like "I can't depend on anybody." But when we say things like that, aren't we really talking about trust?

Once I heard someone say, "I can't trust anybody. I can't even trust myself."

At first I said, "How silly. How could you not trust yourself?" Then I realized after observing people that there is some truth to that statement; and one of the reasons I now believe this to be true is because I do personal training and invariably hear my clients saying, "I don't know what happened. The soda was there. I knew I will regret it later, but I drank it anyway." These are people who knew that what they were doing was detrimental to them, but they could not help themselves, so if we can't even trust ourselves, who or what can we trust?

But let's be real. We can't live a life without trust or without depending on other people. I tried that, and that is called paranoia. I had people working with me, and I continuously overworked myself because I could not trust other people to do as good a job as I would have. How arrogant of me to have that belief.

If we live life that way, we will go absolutely crazy. We won't be able to drive because we won't believe that other people can be as good as us. But paranoia does not have to be real in order for us to respond as if it is real. So what I'm saying is that sometimes, because I had that belief, I made those people less dependable.

However, there are two things you could always depend on. One is pride; people who have pride don't have to be police in order for them to do a good job they police themselves. And the other one is habitual tendencies. You can't always depend on what people say, but their habits are always guaranteed.

WHY I WRITE

I write out of pain.

I write out of happiness.

Pain is a gateway to learning.

That leads me to reflection.

Reflection is a gateway to decision

That leads me to happiness.

Happiness is a gateway to peace.

That leads me to balance.

THE "IN" CROWD

Today, many kids go to school wanting to be with the "in" crowd.

Well, before they go and join the "in" crowd, there are some things I think they should know. And that is the characteristics or the requirements that you need in order to be with the "in" crowd.

Here they are.

In-secure
In-considerate
In-sensitive
In-consistent
Im-mature

Insecure

People who want to be part of the "in" crowd are usually like this because they have the constant need for other people to validate who they are.

Inconsiderate

Because they're insecure, the "in" crowd does not consider the feelings of other people; and they continuously put them down in order to make themselves feel better.

Insensitive

Because they're inconsiderate, they're highly insensitive to people that are not in their immediate circle.

Inconsistent

Because they're insecure, inconsiderate, and insensitive, their trust and loyalty among each other are often inconsistent.

Well, you probably noticed that these words all started with the word "in." Of course, I purposely did that to make a point. You may have also noticed that the last word did not; that was also done on purpose. I did that because if you remove the "in" from those four words, that's what makes a real person and a real friend. The last word, immature, breaks down in two; and that's what we become when we cut the ties from the "in" crowd, "I'm mature." By the way, there's one "in" word that I want you to remember: INDEPENDENT.

THOUGHTS

Today is tomorrow's past.
Let's do our best today so when tomorrow comes
We could talk about "the good old days."

Life itself is amazing.
Therefore, we should be even more amazing.
This way, we won't become a puppet of life.

Walk on the moon with your head on earth.
But don't walk on earth with your head on the moon.

To a winner, reality is yesterday's fantasy.

Winners are those with the ability to act on what they think
about.

WHO IS RESPONSIBLE?

It is not them but I
That is responsible for my failure.
It is not them but I
That is responsible to fulfill my dreams.
It is not them but I
That has to take the action.
It is not them but I
That let their comments break me down.

So if I fail
To take action,
Fail
To fulfill my dreams,
Fail
And allow what they say to break me down,
It is not them but I.

It won't be them but I
That will hold my head high when I get my winning prize.
It won't be them but I
That will have a great big grin when I fulfill my dream.
It won't be them but I
That will feel the satisfaction that comes from taking action to
fulfill my dream.
It won't be them but I
That will forgive their ignorance.

INFLUENCE

A friend of mine got pulled over by a state trooper. He said that the charge was that he was driving under the influence. What this usually means is that you put something in your body that makes you behave in a way that you don't normally behave. In other words, out of control.

But let me ask you. Isn't that the way life really is? Aren't we all a sum of all our past influences? So when you really think about it, we all are driving through life under the influence. But the important thing to find out is what influence we are driving under because ultimately, that influence is driving us.

When I was a child, my mother was always trying to protect me from bad influence. Like any other parent, she wanted to keep me away from the kids who were doing bad things. Not an easy task. She succeeded because she gave me a strong moral background that was not easily shaken, and I think that was the key.

Today, I think that kids fall prey to bad influence because they have a void that they need to fill; that void is low self-esteem, so they do things that they normally would not do to fill that void. They become people pleasers in order to gain instant satisfaction. But it eventually ends up in a long-term turmoil.

Look, it may appear as if my friend's problem is self-inflicted, and you would be right. But that problem did not start there. It started years ago with his low self-esteem, and he began drinking to prove to his friends how cool he was. He was doing it so he could feel like he belongs.

How many kids are going through life that way, trying to impress to get accepted? One thing I always say is people that are externally trying to impress are internally depressed. So the thing for us to do with our kids is to try and fill that void before they go elsewhere to try to fill it.

It is also important for us to be aware of where the influences are coming from; today, we are being bombarded from every angle: television, radio, Internet, and friends. Some people say that we can't pick our children's friends. That may be true, but we can pick where they can go and spend the night. We have to monitor what is happening in our children's lives and guide them.

ALL THAT AND
A BAG OF CHIPS

I remember going to a local restaurant in my town. The lady who owned the restaurant used to give a complimentary bag of chips with every meal. The first time she did it, I told her that I did not order the chips.

She said to me, "Don't worry about it. It comes with the meal. It's free."

I said to her, "That's okay. You can keep it. I don't want it."

She insisted that it was free.

That experience got me thinking about other things in life that come with extra things that we did not ask for or want, particularly, when we enter relationships.

Kids today have an expression when they find someone really attractive. They say, "She's all that and a bag of chips." But when they are saying that, they are really talking about the entrée, you know, the legs, the breasts, etc.

And that will be okay for most people, but if you are allergic to cheese, you better know what's inside a chicken cordon bleu before you order.

Men who choose relationships exactly that way become preoccupied with the parts and pay very little attention to what's inside. And then later on they wonder why they are having a reaction

THE GAME

Some motivational speakers say that life is a game. Well if it is a game then let's play it like a game. More specifically, like a television game. If you ever watch the television game Jeopardy they give you categories and you get to choose which category you want to play. Well in life it should be the same and I use the word should because quite often we don't choose right. One of the reasons for that is because we often choose based on what we think to be true [the obvious] rather than choosing what we should know to be true. By now, you're probably wondering what is this guy talking about, in the TV game if we choose something we don't know anything about our chances of doing well are greatly diminished. So we think. But let me explain, life is a game so play along with me. I'll give you a few categories for you to choose from.

Here are your categories:

Number 1 People that appreciate you.

Number 2 People that don't appreciate you.

Number 3 People that don't know you or care about you one-way or the other.

If you are like most people you probably chose number 1 people that appreciate you. And that's fine but let me ask you this, have you ever been disappointed by someone you thought you knew well and you though they appreciated you? I know I have and after that relationship ends you find out that you really did not know them at all and that it was just a game. That's what I meant by what you think you know. What about the second category people that don't appreciate you. Well, at least you know where they are coming from and their dislike for you would not come as a big surprise. What about number 3? People that don't know you or care about you one way or the other, this may be shocking to some but I believe that the people that achieve the greatest success in life have come from people that they don't know. For example, Stevie Wonder does not know me but I contributed greatly to his success and so have many other people he does not know. The problem with choosing one category is that is one dimensional and in order to do well in the game of life you have to learn to play with all the others because just like in the TV game when you are done with the category you choose to play the other categories still remain and you still have to deal with them.

Sometimes people say I don't have to play. Yes, you could say that but realistically it's not possible because we are all participants in the game of life, yes some may be a passive participant but they are participating nonetheless. For example, I had two of my gymnasts working with me, Maria and Kienan, Maria use to tease Kienan about being a bench warmer for their high school basketball team. The thing is that no matter what the outcome of the game was, Kienan always used the word we when he talked about the game last night. He never separated himself from the team whether he actively plays or was a passive participant. Plus, think about it, televisions game show would not exist if we the passive participant were not watching. Whether we are passive or active participant we both share the same common denominator we all want to win. The plan is to play the game of life like a baseball player try to play his game with the least amount of errors as possible.

CONCLUSIONS

Conclusions are the ending of old ideas and the beginning of new ones.

New ideas are worthless if they are never implemented.

A new thought without action remains just that, a thought.

Keep in mind that action without thought is a dangerous thing.

Think. Act and have a great journey.

Made in the USA
Middletown, DE
04 November 2022

13927270R00038